POLLY AND THE PUFFIN

Jenny COLGAN

POLLY AND THE PUFFIN

LB

THE HAPPY CHRISTMAS

LITTLE, BROWN BOOKS FOR YOUNG READERS

First published in Great Britain in 2017 by Hodder and Stoughton

1 3 5 7 9 10 8 6 4 2

All characters and events in this publication, other than those clearly in the public domain, are fictitious and any resemblance to real persons, living or dead, is purely coincidental.

Adult supervision is recommended with glue, paint, scissors and other sharp points, and for activities that require cooking, baking or heating.

A CIP catalogue record for this book is available from the British Library.

ISBN 9781510200920

Printed in China
The paper and board used in this book are made from wood from responsible sources.

Little, Brown Books for Young Readers
An imprint of Hachette Children's Group
Part of Hodder and Stoughton
Carmelite House, 50 Victoria Embankment
London EC4Y 0DZ

An Hachette UK Company
www.hachette.co.uk

www.hachettechildrens.co.uk

To Lucia and Bethan

Polly is a little girl who lives by the sea.

She has a puffin friend called Neil.

He says, "Eep!"

Neil and Polly had seen lots and lots of adverts for Christmas toys and lots of decorations in the windows.

"Is it Christmas yet?" said Polly.

"Not yet, it's only November," said Mummy.

"It must be Christmas tomorrow?" said Polly. "Or maybe the day after?"

"Nope," said Daddy. "Afraid not."

"But we have been practising for the nativity play. Neil is in it."

"Eep," said Neil.

"There is Gold, Frankincense and Bird," Polly explained.

"I'm not sure that's right," Daddy said.

"Let's not start this again," said Mummy.

"Neil thinks it's Christmas now," said Polly.

"Eep," agreed Neil.

"It's not Christmas now," said Mummy. "But if you are very good, soon we shall go up to the big city and you can visit Santa."

Polly liked this idea very much. She and Neil did their best to be good.

They tidied up their toys.

They went down to visit Celeste, Neil's puffin girlfriend. She was sitting on her and Neil's egg. She did not like Polly very much.

They wrote their Christmas lists.

On Polly's list was: a raccoon tree house, some puffin pyjamas and a new bow tie for Neil as he had eaten the last one.

On Neil's list was: a fish, some cereal and his hatched egg.

"AND NOW WE ARE READY TO MEET SANTA!" said Polly.

"Puffins can't come to the city," said Mummy. "They might get lost and have to go live in the zoo."

Polly and Neil were not happy.

CHRISTMAS
DECORATIONS

"Why don't you take Wrong Puffin?" said Mummy.

Wrong Puffin was Polly's special toy puffin for when Neil was busy.

"Because he is stupid and not much use and we hate him," said Polly.

"Eep!" said Neil.

"Polly and Neil, be polite!" said Mummy.

So Polly put Wrong Puffin and her Christmas list in her backpack.

Neil was not impressed. He flew out of the window.

"Where's Neil going?" said Mummy.

"He's probably going to sit on the egg with Celeste," said Polly. "When will it hatch? We've been waiting for such a long time."

"I don't know," said Polly's mummy. "The lady from the puffin sanctuary said that the egg was early because the weather has been warm."

"It's not warm now," said Polly.

"I know," said Mummy. "But nobody knows quite when the puffling will arrive."

"I think I would like it to come today," said Polly. "I don't like waiting."

"Sometimes," said Mummy, "waiting is the best part."

Polly wasn't sure about that.

The nearest big city was called Edinburgh.

It was very dark and cold and busy and full of lights and buses and people. Polly found it very exciting, but a bit scary too.

"There are LOTS of raincoats," she said.

"There are," said Polly's mummy.

Finally they reached a huge shop. Polly loved the bright, shiny window displays with toys that moved.

"It's beautiful," she said.

"It is," said her mummy, even though the rain was going down the neck of her coat.

They watched the window for a little while, and Polly's mummy gave her a cuddle, just like the one I'm giving you now.

Inside the shop it was very crowded and busy and there was a long wait to see Santa.

Suddenly, Polly felt shy. She pulled Wrong Puffin out of her bag and gave him a cuddle.

Now what would you like?" asked Santa when it was Polly's turn. He had a kind face and a big furry coat. Polly's voice got very small.

"I would like . . ."

Polly pulled out her list.

But she had brought Neil's list by mistake. Oh no!

Polly and Santa were quiet for a little while. Polly looked down at the paper. She felt all hot and wanted to cry.

"Um? Fish?" she said in a tiny voice.

"And some cereal? And . . . an egg?"

Santa didn't say anything for a bit.

"An egg?" he said. "Like a chocolate egg?"

"A puffin egg?" said Polly. Her cheeks were very, very red. "And a puffling to hatch?"

"Well," said Santa, rubbing his chin. "I will certainly mention it to the elves and see what they can do."

Then he let her choose a little present from his sack.

And then Polly went back to Mummy and burst into tears.

"I GAVE SANTA THE WRONG LIST!" she said.

"I gave Santa Neil's list! He's going to bring me a fish for Christmas!!!"

Mummy put her arm around Polly.

"Don't worry," she said. "We'll figure this out. Santa is very smart. Shall we go home and have some hot chocolate?"

And that is what they did.

That night, Neil was too busy helping Celeste with their egg to come and play.

Wrong Puffin was nowhere to be found.

And Polly was very, very worried about her Christmas list.

She wrote a new one and they sent it up the chimney, but Polly wasn't sure it would get to Santa.

Daddy made special hot chocolate with marshmallows.

"I was rude to Wrong Puffin," Polly said. "That was why he got lost."

"It's not your fault, Polly. Toys just do get lost sometimes," said Mummy. "I'll phone the shop tomorrow and see if he's been handed in."

TEA

That night the wind blew hard around the little house by the sea, and there was no Neil and there was no Wrong Puffin.

Polly slept with Neil's box on her head. It didn't help.

The next day Polly was still sad, and Neil still was too busy to play with her!

It was not looking like a very good Christmas.

There was a carol concert at school. Neil only came in at the end for the FA LA LAs. Then he went away again, and Polly didn't have Wrong Puffin to keep her company while he was gone.

There was a nativity in the village.

There was gold, frankincense and bird, just like Polly and Neil had practised.

But Neil was a bad wise man and Did Not Behave.

They decorated the Christmas tree in the little house by the sea. Polly wanted to have fun, but the puffin decorations made her feel even sadder.

Christmas was going all wrong!

Finally it was Christmas Eve
and Polly managed to be
just a little bit excited.

"Come here," said Mummy. And they all sat by the fire and read the story of Christmas.

"I like stories about babies coming," said Polly.

"Good," said Mummy.

As Polly slept, the stars came out and the earth grew still. And at midnight all the animals went quiet, because they knew that it was Christmas, too.

In the morning, Polly woke up and it was Christmas day!

Waiting for her downstairs there was a brown parcel, tied up with string, all the way from Edinburgh. Polly opened it up to find Wrong Puffin – wearing a smart bow tie – and a new fluffy puffling toy!

And there was a raccoon tree house too, because Santa does in fact get notes that go up the chimney.

And on the steps by the back door there was a little black feather. Polly always knew what that meant.

Polly rushed to find Neil's presents. Then she and Mummy and Daddy put on their coats, and climbed the steps to the lighthouse.

There, they found Neil and Celeste and . . .

. . . a brand new baby puffling,
born on Christmas morning!

They weren't allowed to touch the new baby so Polly left the presents nearby.

They didn't know if the puffling was a boy or a girl. So Polly decided to call it Vyvian, which is a very good name for a boy *or* a girl.

Everything that was lost had been found and the world felt new . . .

And everyone had a VERY happy Christmas day.

POLLY AND NEIL

Did you know?

The world's largest Christmas stocking was created in Italy in 2011 – it was 51.35m long.

Nearly 60 MILLION Christmas trees are grown each year in Europe.

Christmas pudding was originally a sort of porridge made with wine and raisins.

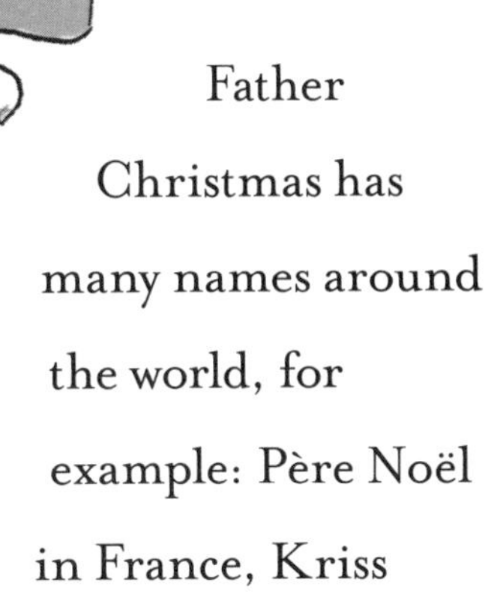

Father Christmas has many names around the world, for example: Père Noël in France, Kriss Kringle in Germany, Święty Mikolaj in Poland and Babbo Natale in Italy.

The first snowmen were made by people to ward off evil winter spirits, but now they're just a fun way to play in the snow!

Christmas Jokes

Q. What do you call Father Christmas at the beach?

A. *Sandy* Claus!

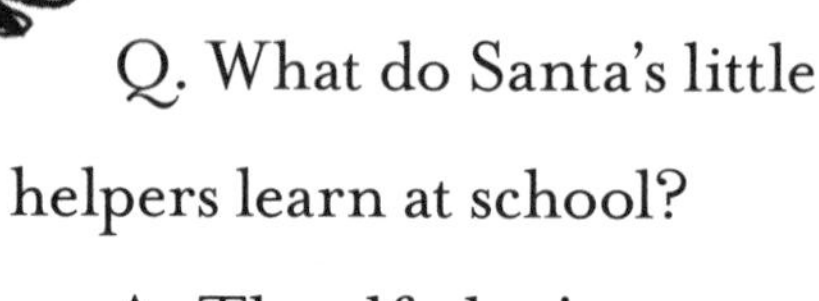

Q. What do Santa's little helpers learn at school?

A. The elf-abet!

Q. What do you get when you cross a vampire with a snowman?

A. Frostbite!

Q. What do you call a reindeer with lots of snow in its ears?

A. Anything you want – he can't hear you!

Q. What do snowmen wear on their heads?

A. Ice caps!

Q. What do you get if you cross a Christmas tree with an apple?

A. A pineapple!

RECIPES

Christmas Biscuits for Your Tree

Neil loves these decorations because when nobody is looking he can eat them straight from the tree! You'll need a grown-up to help you with this recipe – they can do all the parts involving the oven.

INGREDIENTS

- 335g butter
- 400g dark brown sugar
- 1 egg
- 480g plain flour
- 2 teaspoons cinnamon
- 1 teaspoon nutmeg
- ½ teaspoon cloves
- ¼ teaspoon bicarbonate of soda
- Ribbon/thread/string for hanging

INSTRUCTIONS

1. Pre-heat your oven to 180°C.
2. Cream butter and sugar together thoroughly.
3. Add egg and beat until light and fluffy.
4. Sift together the flour, spices and bicarbonate of soda and stir into the mixture.
5. Chill the mixture for at least 2 hours.
6. Sprinkle a little flour on a work surface and roll out the mixture to about 5mm thick before cutting out using your favourite biscuit cutters.

7. Then, using a skewer or a blunt pencil, make a good-sized hole in each biscuit.
8. Carefully using a spatula, lay the biscuits on a baking sheet and cook in the oven for 12 minutes or until golden brown.
9. Leave the biscuit s to cool on the baking sheet for 10 minutes before removing.
10. When the biscuits are fully cool, thread ribbon through each hole and hang on your Christmas tree!

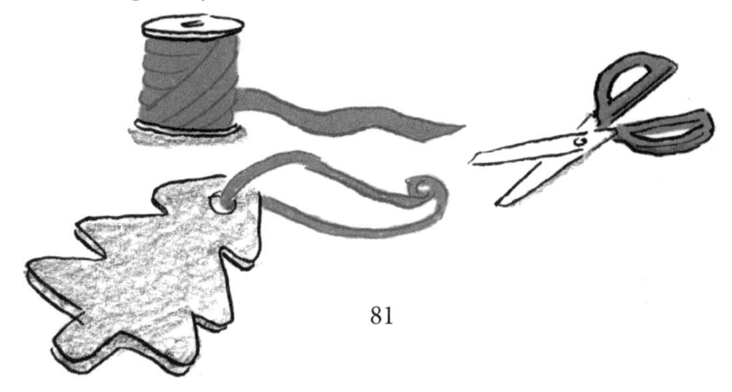

Mince Pies for Santa

Polly loves cooking, but sometimes she can be a little impatient when things take a long time. So this is one of her favourite Christmas recipes because it's so quick! You will need a grown-up to help you, especially with putting the pies in the oven.

INGREDIENTS

- 250g jar of mincemeat
- 500g block of pre-made shortcrust pastry
- 1 egg
- Plain flour
- Butter/margarine

INSTRUCTIONS

1. Pre-heat your oven to 200°C.

2. Take a non-stick cupcake tin with 12 holes, and grease with butter/margarine.

3. Sprinkle flour on your work surface and then roll out your pastry to about 3mm thick (similar to a pound coin!).

4. Using a biscuit cutter which is larger than the cupcake holes (about 8cm wide should be good), stamp out 12 circles. Then put them in the cupcake tin.

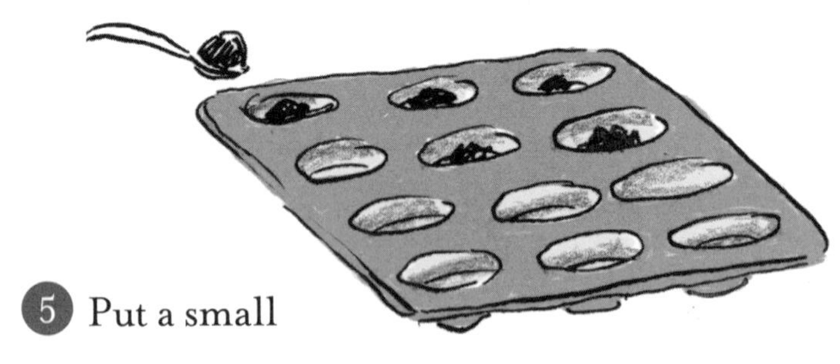

5. Put a small spoonful of mincemeat in each one –

careful not to put in too much or it will bubble over!

6 Re-roll the leftover pastry and use a smaller biscuit cutter – either a circle or a fun shape like a star – to cut out the tops of your pies and place over the mincemeat.

7 Beat the egg and use this to brush the tops of the pies so they turn nice and golden.

8 Bake for 15-20 minutes and leave to cool slightly before eating! (Polly likes hers with ice-cream!)

ACTIVITIES

Festive Baubles

Take a look at these shiny baubles! This one is Polly's favourite one to hang on her tree – can you colour it in?

This one is ready for you to decorate in any way you'd like.

Making Snow Globes

Polly made one of these with a little plastic puffin toy inside, but you could use any plastic toy that's small enough to fit in a jar!

You will need:

- A clean, empty jar (a jam or other food jar would work well)
- A small plastic toy
- Heavy-duty glue
- Glycerine (find this in the baking aisle at the supermarket, or online)
- Glitter

- Boiled (then cooled completely!) water – enough to fill the jar

INSTRUCTIONS

1. Ask a grown-up to help you stick your toy to the inside of the jar's lid – leave to dry for at least ten minutes.
2. Fill the jar with cooled water, then add a small squirt of glycerine and a pinch of glitter.
3. Carefully screw the lid back on – being careful not to knock the toy as you do so.
4. Turn the jar upside-down so it's standing on its lid – give it a little shake to make the glitter swirl!

Make a Snowman

Ask a grown-up to help you trace or photocopy this design onto a white piece of card. Cut around the shapes and also down the central line. Then you can slide the two pieces together and decorate! This makes a good decoration, or could even be given as a 3D Christmas card.

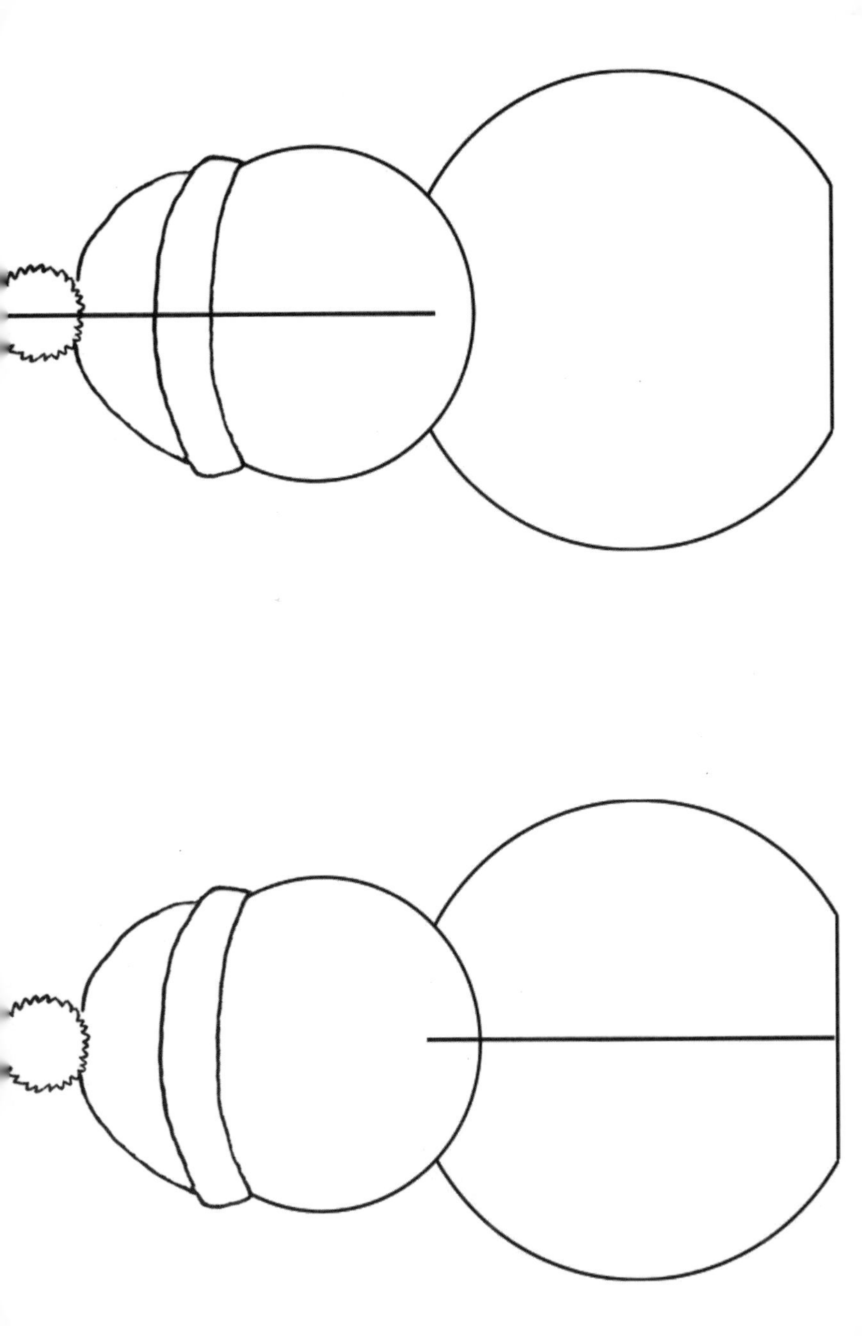

Jenny Colgan is best known for writing bestselling novels for grown-ups including *Meet Me at the Cupcake Café* and *Welcome to Rosie Hopkins' Sweetshop of Dreams*. But when a feathery character from *Little Beach Street Bakery* caught her readers' attention she knew he needed a story of his own . . .

Thomas Docherty is an acclaimed author and illustrator of children's picture books including *Little Boat*,

Big Scary Monster and *The Driftwood Ball*. *The Snatchabook*, which was written by his wife Helen, has been shortlisted for several awards in the UK and the US and translated into 17 languages. He loves going into schools and helping kids to write their own stories. Thomas lives in Wales by the sea with his wife and two young daughters, so he had plenty of inspiration when it came to illustrating *Polly and the Puffin*.

Neil can't believe he's in so many books now! He has a cameo in several of Jenny's adult books, and four with Polly. Take a look over the page to see if you've read them all . . .

Have you read Polly and Neil's other books?